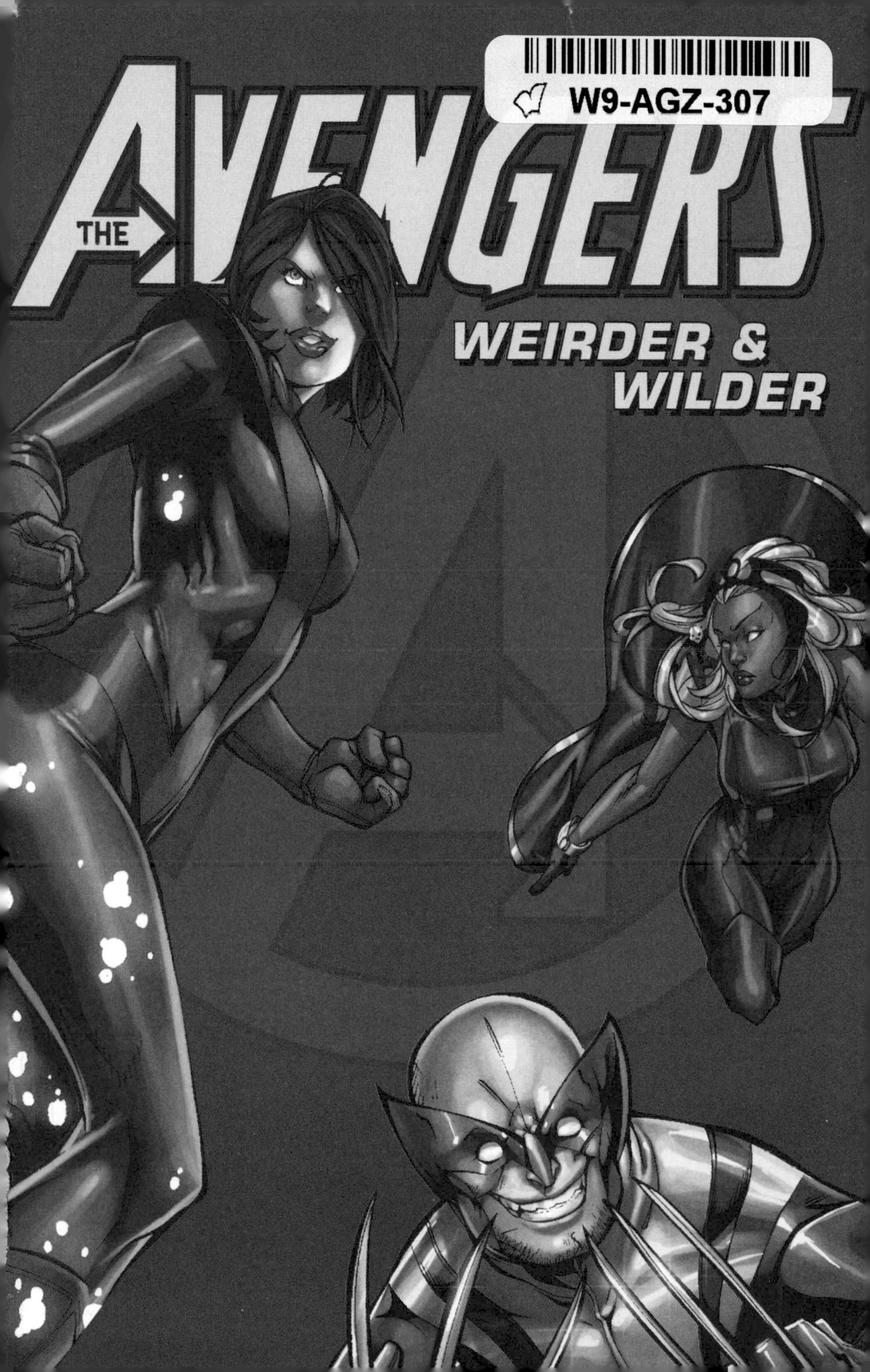
THE AVENGERS
WEIRDER & WILDER

THE

NGERS

WEIRDER & WILDER

Writers: Jeff Parker & Paul Tobin
Pencils: Ig Guara
Inks: Jay Leisten & Sandro Ribeiro

Colors: Ulises Arreola & Guillem Mari
Letters: Dave Sharpe
Cover Art: Leonard Kirk, Terry Pallot, William Baumann & Guru eFX
Assistant Editor: Nathan Cosby
Editor: Mark Paniccia

Captain America created by Joe Simon & Jack Kirby

Collection Editor: Jennifer Grünwald
Editorial Assistant: Alex Starbuck
Assistant Editors: Cory Levine & John Denning
Editor, Special Projects: Mark D. Beazley
Senior Editor, Special Projects: Jeff Youngquist
Senior Vice President of Sales: David Gabriel
Vice President of Creative: Tom Marvelli

Editor in Chief: Joe Quesada
Publisher: Dan Buckley

#24

CAPTAIN AMERICA
STORM
SPIDER-MAN
GIANT-GIRL
WOLVERINE
ANT-MAN
NEW YORK CITY...
Listen up kids. Spider-Man here with a cautionary tale for you.
There was a tragic time in Avengers history recently--when hero turned against hero. Teamwork had broken down.
That's why we want you to pay attention, so you don't go down that road. It's a cautionary tale, to get across our message...
Shut--
NNNNNK!
SUPER-SOLDIER FROM WORLD WAR II. WEATHER GODDESS. SPIDER-POWERED WEB-SLINGER. GIANT-SIZED CRIMEFIGHTER. FERAL MUTANT BRAWLER. PINT-SIZED SCIENTIST. TOGETHER THEY ARE THE WORLD'S MIGHTIEST HEROES, BATTLING THE FOES THAT NO SINGLE SUPER HERO COULD WITHSTAND!
THE AVENGERS
DON'T BE HATIN'.
Jeff Parker writer Ig Guara pencils Jay Leisten inks Ulises Arreola color
Dave Sharpe letters Irene Lee production Kirk & Baumann cover
Nathan Cosby assistant editor Mark Paniccia editor Joe Quesada editor in chief Dan Buckley publisher

I... wanted... PHO!
Don't do it!
Take yer best shot!
Like using that healing factor, huh, Wolverine?
Ah... Giant-Girl? What are you doing with that truck?
I... don't know. Trying to keep our team in the shade?
Team, I'm sorry if I injured any of you. I don't know what came over me.
Me neither, Cap. We were all just trying to figure out where to go for lunch and things just...
...escalated.
Avengers!
Mayor Burrini, hello.
Aren't you supposed to protect us? Or is your mission statement to wreck the city fighting amongst yourselves now?
Look at this street!
"The mayor yelled at us for a few more minutes, and then slapped us with some public service duty to make up for the mess.

"We went back to our head-quarters and remembered why we'd gone out in the first place.
"We were overseeing a new criminal work release program at Stark Tower."
These convicts are still hogging the cafeteria.
It's worth it. This program will channel the skills of people who work for super-villains into useful roles in society. Especially safeguarding us from attacks.
Hey look, everybody, it's Karl! How's my favorite evil henchman.
Spider-Bro! I'm lovin' working here at the Tower, it's the best.
Hey, sorry about that whole M.O.D.O.C.-head thing.
No problem! Good luck in the lab.
Thanks for the chance! I'm going to make you guys proud of me!
Yeah you will! Where's a table?
So did you figure out why we had that mysterious rage?
No, but they brought out some more tater tots.
Really?

We're too powerful to lose control, we--
And that was the dilemma the Avengers faced. Would they ultimately save the world? Or *destroy* it!
What are you doing?
I'm filming our public service announcement about rage for the city. A news crew gave me tape of our embarrassing fight today!
Great.
I'm going to go back and dub in my narration every-where, since you can't see my mouth move.
Just edit out all the parts where you reveal all our secret identities.
No, wait, *I'll* edit it.
Good tots.
The orzo here is what I like, but they never give you enough.
Fortunately, I can *make* it enough.

Wait, now how does that work? Will you still be full when you return to normal size?
Glmbmfmf.

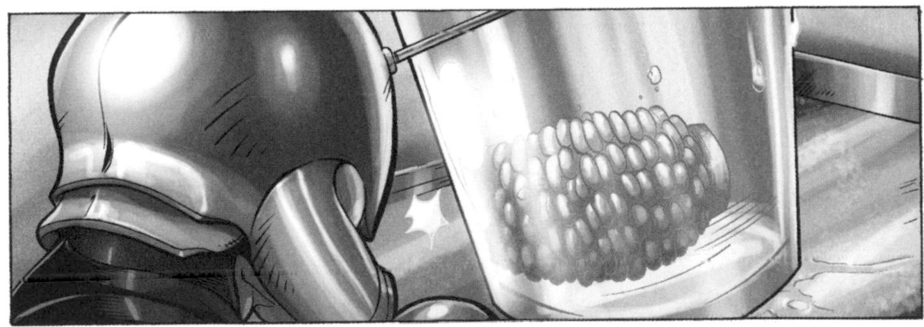

SPDONK!
Close one!

My pudding!
SPLATZ
Twerp!
CLINK
FLMGH!
BZZZ BZZZ BZZZ
BZZZ BZZZ BZZZ
Agh! OW-OW!
You brought those stupid ants of yours in here?!
Ha!
What's so funny!
SWAK

Why'd ya have to wreck lunch?
Oogh!
Captain America was the one who started it--with his corn!
I'm tired of all this childishness! Why is everyone but me so stupid?!
That's the way we ate our lunch back in the war! We rolled it first!
I learned it...from you! Okay!?!

It's all going to plan. And it's a good plan.

AVENGERS' HEADQUARTERS ATOP STARK TOWER...
We soon came to our senses, but team morale was going down. And I never got to eat my pudding.
AVENGERS TOO HOSTILE?
We've got to do something about this, this is insane!
I am, I'm calling Bruce.
What? I don't think the Hulk is going to help that much...
No, just Bruce Banner. His whole life is about trying to deal with anger.
And failing miserably at it.
Bruce Banner A.K.A. The Incredible Hulk.
Really? Well, then I'm not coming down there, I don't want to get angry too.
Because I just got a new suit. Yes, it's purple--look, if I can make a suggestion...
Okay, everyone, into Quinjet 1.
We're going to...
...the doctor.
And that's one to grow on!

"Bruce sent us all to his therapist, a psychologist named Doc Samson.
"He once tried to stop the process that turns Bruce into The Hulk, and was irradiated with gamma energy too, giving him incredible strength and green arena-rock hair."
Good to meet you all. First I'd like you to fill out these profiles and then I'll ask you each some questions.
...so you felt that...*ants*... were the key to fighting evil.
They were just so orderly, so purposeful.
Reverse Napoleon complex
I want you to express yourself through this clay.
Um...clay really sticks to my fingers...
Emotionally stunted, immature, needs a wife.
In my last dream I created rain for a farming village and they made a statue of me.
Superiority complex
Single...?

Say the first word that comes into your mind. Star.
Flag.
Ring.
Freedom.
Lady.
Liberty.
Currently there is no danger present, yet you choose to stay giant-sized. Why do you think that is?
Uh, well...
Some pretty flowers.
"The Doc kept us in there for hours, and then finally gave us his prescription...
"Go get in a fight."
Like firemen or soldiers, you're primarily assembled for big action. When you don't have an outlet to channel all your great power, you become restless.
I think as a unit you're manifesting a crisis to have some-thing to battle. My suggestion: Be proactive. Find a real threat to be the focus of this aggression.

Wow, I feel better already!
Yeah, I hate you all a lot less! But what if we can't find a villain for our therapy?
Don't worry.

Our satellite scans and intel have approximated what is likely the latest base of Hydra, the largest criminal organization in the world!
Perfect.

The best defense is a good offense. Why should we wait for them to implement a new scheme?
We're on the way.

"Sure enough, Hydra was up to no good. It's in their mission statement, after all."
The Bi-Beast is nearly ready, Hydra Leader! His synthetic strength rivals that of the Hulk!
I will be more interested when *five* of the models are completed.
The next time we face The Avengers or S.H.I.E.L.D., I want them to be completely outgunned and overwhelmed!
Well, he does have *two* heads.
DE-STROY..

Got him!
BZZZZAKKK
We're under attack!
RRYAAHH!!
Who wants to taste the curb?!
Come on, let's get it out!
Don't cage the rage!

We haven't even begun our latest operation! We...
...we weren't ready!!
KAPOW!
Well boo hoo! Sorry we're early!
We're trying to become self-actualized!
All right! They're fighting back!
YARR!!
WOOORGH!
Breadbasket!

Yaahh!!
No! That's the head that deals with rampages!
I'll get that second noggin.
But that's the one that concentrates on crushing our enemies!
SHWOIP!
Hey! That was mine!
I *called* that head!
I didn't hear you.
Are those not real ears stickin' outside your mask?
This therapy isn't working.

When is Ant-Man going to land the Quinjet already?
I already did! And thanks for not saving me a villain to fight! Jerks!
CLOMP
That one's not completely unconscious.
Oh, well thank you.
Wait, who's in Quinjet 2?
I bet it's Iron Man. He saw the bill from Doc Samson and is freaking out.
'Course it's gonna be a lot, he analyzed six people!
Are you going to chip in?
'Course not.

He's not sticking me with the bill!
Especially since it didn't work--I'm angrier than ever!
I got that righteous anger that's really scary when you think about it!
You guys are amateurs!
Look, you morons! It's not Iron Man, someone stole our B ship!
Which makes me quite angry!

Yeah, you're feelin' it now.
You all got out of range of my Hate Ray, so I borrowed one of your jets to bring it to you.
Name's *Hate-Monger.* So come on now...
...let's get some *hate* up in here!
So *that's* who's monging all the hate.
You've been playin' us all along?

As Doc Samson would say, let me express how I feel about that.
That's cool, get it out. But first...
...why you been telling everyone Giant-Girl's getting fat?
I KNEW IT!
WHUMP
Don't get too uppity, G-Girl...
...after what you said about Storm's "dancer" hair.
What about my hair!
AAGGHHH!!!

That Storm is the kind of hero I like!
Well, except for her weird tendency...

...to badmouth the U.S.A...
Oh really.
UNFH!

You idiots! All you have to do is take out that guy!
Forget it, all I need is three ants, and--

THUMP
OW! You shot that little nerd right in my eye!
Just cry him out, Shorty.

That tears it! You're history!

Give it up, punk!

Boy, your senses are going bad--you can't land a web anymore.
Course I can, I just landed two.

You're the one who didn't notice that I'm holding myself back with my leg.

Idiot.
THWAANNG

This is the worst team I've ever been on!
If you punks took orders like we did back in the war--
Hey, stop!
I have her!
You also have horrible dandruff.
That's snow and you know it!

Take it back! You always think your hair is better than mine--
I do not!
Well it is! It's so shiny and manageable, even in a fight--
Well, I'm envious of your uniform.
Really? Gosh...
What's with them?
Maybe... they're gonna...
They're not angry, that's what!
That must mean...
...aw, shoot, come on...
BZZZ
BZZZ
His hate ray is inoperational! Get him!

Now we'll see what's what.
Dang it...
KARL?!
Yeah, it's me. I'm the Hate-Monger.
But why?
I've worked for all the big evil organizations. And I got to thinking.
Uh-oh.
AIM... HYDRA...The Serpent Society...none of them paid so great. And benefits? Forget it.
"Yet there was all this, like, undying loyalty. Part of that was fear of torture, sure. But there was something else.
"I noticed that the main thing that unified those groups... was hate."
This will be the end of Captain America!
Hear hear!
Boo heroes!
"The hate kept them a tight unit. I used a lot of their medical records to calculate a way to stimulate the emotion with a wavelength."

I thought I could achieve the goals of the Work Release Program by making you guys a tighter group. Then I took the role of the Hate-Monger to give you a common enemy.
The problem there? We already have *lots* of common enemies.
And we already work together well! You actually endangered that teamwork.
We've learned a valuable lesson today. Trust no one.
That's not the lesson.
Your first mistake was having an idea.
Your second was acting on that idea.
It wasn't a total waste of time. We nipped a Hydra base in the bud.
And now you're going to work with us to make sure the frequency can be defended against. If anyone else comes up with this technology, they could launch whole wars!
No prob. I think we can do it, though it's pretty hard to stop. Except for Wolverine, of course. His healing factor kept warding it off.
Wait.
You mean all this time Wolverine wasn't actually being affected by the frequency?
Ha!
Good times.
THE END

#25

SPIDER-POWERED WEB-SLINGER. SUPER-STRONG ALTER EGO OF SCIENTIST BRUCE BANNER. WEATHER GODDESS. PINT-SIZED SCIENTIST. FERAL MUTANT BRAWLER. SUPER-SOLDIER FROM WORLD WAR II. BRILLIANT ARMORED INVENTOR. GIANT-SIZED CRIMEFIGHTER. TOGETHER THEY ARE THE WORLD'S MIGHTIEST HEROES, BATTLING THE FOES THAT NO SINGLE SUPER HERO COULD WITHSTAND!
THE AVENGERS
SPIDER-MAN?
HULK?
STORM?
ANT-MAN?
WOLVERINE?
CAPTAIN AMERICA?
IRON MAN?
GIANT-GIRL?
Manhattan...
You gentlemen can go ahead and surrender now.
I knew there was some reason we weren't supposed to do this in New York.
Told you we should have brought the whole Wrecking Crew!
WHO WANTS TO BE A (DIFFERENT) SUPER HERO?
JEFF PARKER--WRITER IG GUARA--PENCILER
SANDRO RIBEIRO--INKER ULISES ARREOLA--COLORIST
DAVE SHARPE--LETTERER KIRK & GURU EFX--COVER JOE SABINO--PRODUCTION
NATHAN COSBY--ASSISTANT EDITOR MARK PANICCIA--EDITOR
JOE QUESADA--EDITOR IN CHIEF DAN BUCKLEY--PUBLISHER

Aw, missed. But you really put a hurtin' on my teammate *Column-Man*.
Shut up!
SKABASCHHH
Wow. You're going up against the world's most advanced weapons system with a crowbar?
Well... yeah! I guess...
ZWHIP
Here's our offer. If you lug that money back into the vault so I don't have to, I promise I'll avoid the faces.
ZWHOOOOOOOO...
What is... do you hear this strange noise?
It's so...

ZWWWAANANNZZZZ

Uh...hey...
I'm a...Iron Man,
right?
Whoa! I'm
Wolverine, dog!
Check out these
sweet claws!
Got him!
Ha ha!
Ow.
I'll
take care
of this!
I'll get so
big, I'll just...
stomp 'em!
That'll stop
those bums.
Because I-am-
GI-ANT-
GIRRRLLL!!!

KRONGCCHH
NNK
Good try, Katy--I mean, G-Girl!
I'll just make them eat a force ray.
Eat it, hoods!
WWMMMPPP
...can-he... walk at all, if he mo-oves will he fall...
Oh shoot, that's the radio...
Didn't you guys used to be... competent?
We are! I'm the Iron Man, dude!
...nobody wants him--he just stares at the wo-orld...
Man, this is turning out to be a great day.
WHOOMP

BSH
See, I think this was the most punishing blow he took.
No, maybe that was.
KRAK!
Ouch!
Iron Man and Giant-Girl are doing okay, but they'll be in the medical ward for a while. Concussions, cracked ribs.
Wolverine has his healing factor, so he's fine. I'm looking at data from the Iron Man armor to figure out what happened.
Turn that junk off!
I don't remember any of that!
Of course not, look how hard you got hit. Dag.
That's not me fighting! We all blacked out, like I said!
It sure looks like you.
I'm warning ya! Turn the news off now!
Okay, okay.
KLIK!

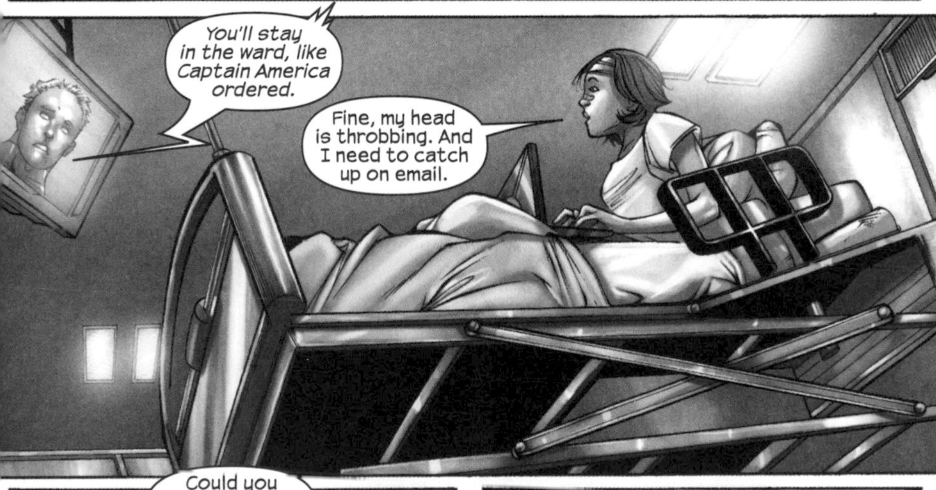

SUBJECT: WANT TO BE **SOMEONE ELSE?**

IMAGINE THAT YOU COULD SWITCH PLACES WITH **ANYONE** IN THE WORLD. RUN A COUNTRY. PLA
BASKETBALL. PILOT A SHUTTLECRAFT. BE A SUPER HERO.

...and I just saw one that raises a red flag.

Upstate New York.
Hello, I'm Juno. Thank you for the non-refundable deposit.
And for referring so many of your eligible friends!
My associates and I thought it might be a fun group activity.
Storm said "fun."
Then follow me and I'll show you just what we can offer.
These clients are living out their dreams. Obviously becoming a heavy-weight champion or hip-hop diva demands many sacrifices--but here at Zola, you need only give up money to become them for a short time.
I'm gonna beat him so bad, he's gonna hate it. He will not like it!
I deserve all the Grammys! Country too!
Once the desired host is targeted by our equipment, the client's cerebral network is imposed onto it, while that person's is transferred here.
While a day as a celebrity is the norm, we do offer specials for a whole weekend.
And we will not hesitate to invade and launch missiles and stuff.

Isn't this kind of... unethical?
Ethical...hmm. I'll talk to our customer service department about that and get back to you.
In the meantime, here is the best person to answer any more questions...
Our founder and the mastermind behind the mindhosting process--
Arnim Zola!
Thanks, Juno. Welcome.
Arnim Zola... of course! Weren't you arrested in Switzerland for conducting experiments on college students?
Ah...that must be another Arnim Zola. Hey, how would you like to be an astronaut on the space station?
No, I was thinking I might like to be a super hero. Can you do that?
Of course, we just let three clients be members of The Avengers the other day!
Uh, calm down, Bruce.
Oh really. Could you switch out the brain of say...
--Wolverine???
That's the easiest one, not much to transfer at all.

YHRAAAAHHH!
POP
Uh, dude. You knocked his head off.
Getting... upset...
Oh please. Do you think I would leave the world's greatest mind where it might be hit by a ruffian like him?
My head is in a secret location guarded by charged-particle cannons. I knew when we scheduled your group something was suspicious.
I think we better get into our work duds, folks.

I have prepared for this confrontation!
You are not messing with some chimp like The Leader or a defective such as M.O.D.O.C.! I am the greatest mind the world will ever know--but never understand!
I AM ARNIM ZOLA!
Okay, we totally underestimated you, guy.
If we had known you were the kind of villain who would remove his head and put a plasma screen in his chest, we would have really rethought all this.
That is--
--ENOUGH!

Soon...
What happened? Did we shut down the Zola business and then all go take a nap in the woods?
No. You have been through my cerebral transference and brought outside. I don't want any damage to my building as my newly hired bodyguards deal with you.
What body-guards?
You may remember them from yesterday's skirmish at the bank...the Wrecking Crew?
Except now we have the whole crew.
And we're gonna beat the snot outta *you.*
Gol-dang!
Nice rhyme, guys. Nice!

I've always wanted to flatten the Hulk!
Indeed, Bulldozer, indeed.
OOUGH!

Save some for me! Y'all hogged all the fun for yourselves yesterday, day nab it!
You were napping, Piledriver! You snooze, you lose, you know that.

And while we're half-conscious, you chumps look pretty big.
But now you're going to catch a serious beating!
RRRAAAAARRRR!!!!
Um... don't hurt yourself, little dude!

Come on Avengers, let's use our brains!

Hey friends, I could use some help! How about I put a few hundred of you on The Wrecker's shoulder and you crawl in his ear. Then I'm going to go jump on Thunderball's eye--
Spidey, what are you doing?

I'm tying up our favorite evil demolition team, what else?
Huh. Must be out.

I'll just be a sec, guys, I need to recharge--
--whoop--
--UNGH!
Of course. His mind has been replaced by Spider-Man's! Well played, Zola.
Yet I shall now summon the elements upon your hired hands and you will be forced to restore him.
Skies, answer!
Aw man, how great *is* this?
YEE-HAW!
This is jes' like whompin' critters in the henhouse!
WHOMMP

Puny wrecking crew! Hulk will show you who is best at smashing!
Oh please, Zola, make it stop! This is too much!

Laugh this off!
SLAMMMM
I'm still pretty good at hitting a target!
And Cap doesn't have all the proportional spider-strength I'm used to--
--but this crowbar evens things up a bit.
WHANG
Back atcha, Captain Spider.
Thanks, T-ball.
WHOMP

Grr!!! Smash! SMASHH!!!
Now let's-- hey, will somebody get Hulk off me?
I'm the best there is at what I do, and what I do is--
I'll get that. Night, Hulk.
Hulk not like! --uhh.
TAP
Do not tarry, they could adjust to their new bodies! Eliminate them quickly!
What's "tarry" mean?
Got this one.
SWAT

Hey, we... won.
Hot dang! Let's hog-tie 'em and drive around with 'em on the car!
You see men, power alone is nothing if you do not know how to use it.

Very true, Zola. That's why I didn't charge into battle with an untested body.
Now I think I have the hang of being Wolverine.
How nice. I have the hang of flattening Wolverine, so that's perfect.

BOOOMM
One down.
Oh, my bad, Bulldozer!

That's enough of that ball.
Took me forever to figure out how these pop out.
SLASH
Aw *naw!* Not my chain!

Hope ya got Wolverine's healin' power too, old man!
Wait. No, I don't.
AAGGHH!
Wait fer me! I kin flatten 'im out like johnnycake!
Piledriver, what backwater did you grow up in?
Ah, foul. I knew we were missing one.
Aha! Found you!
BBAAABBBOOOOMMMMM

Sorry I've been gone so long! I'm having a hard time adjusting to this much muscle. I overleapt into several counties trying to return.
Captain?
...yes...
...grits and gravy, collard greens...
It appears only the Wrecker and I are left to decide the bout, and now I can work this body.
Whew. Don't worry Zola, I think I can take 'im. Her.
I'm not worried.
I *know* you can.
ZHWWAAAAAANNZZZ
Now you have the more powerful form. Please put Storm out of service.
Yeah--I feel like I can lift the planet! Sweet!

Go on, end it!
Okay, but...
THWIP
But what?
I mean... that's me! I gotta get back in that body later.
What if I mess me up too bad?
Finally figured out how to work these webs!
But what I really need is this...
Like this?
Stop! Not my face!
WHAK
This is ridiculous, we're so close to victory!
Very well...
ZWWWAAAAAANNNZZZ

Hey! I'm back!
What? That's not the switch I was making...
The end.
No!!!
Zola, you had better comply.
No! I'll switch your mind with... will one of my men please wake up!
We interrupt this nutty villain for a special announcement: The Avengers win!
What! Get out of here! What is this?
I've pirated your signal, Zola!
Now if this works the way it looks like, I think I can put my team back together...

THE VAULT.
Super-prisoner confinement facility.

Gol-Dang it.

That takes care of the Wrecking Crew, now what?

Now we've got to trace these signals and go arrest Arnim Zola's head.

We had better do it soon. I don't think it's good for them to watch too much television.

Yay, Hulk's favorite!

This is a rerun.

Point his right arm back up more.

More...

THE END

#26

CAPTAIN AMERICA
STORM
SPIDER-MAN
GIANT-GIRL
ANT-MAN
HULK
The reports were right! Extra-terrestrials have invaded India!
I knew all those telemarketing call centers were going to push someone over the edge!
SUPER-SOLDIER FROM WORLD WAR II. WEATHER GODDESS. SPIDER-POWERED WEB-SLINGER. GIANT-SIZED CRIMEFIGHTER. PINT-SIZED SCIENTIST. SUPER STRONG ALTER EGO OF SCIENTIST BRUCE BANNER TOGETHER THEY ARE THE WORLD'S MIGHTIEST HEROES, BATTLING THE FOES THAT NO SINGLE SUPER HERO COULD WITHSTAND!
THE AVENGERS
PARADIGM SHIFT
Jeff Parker writer Ig Guara pencils Sandro Ribeiro inks Ulises Arreola color
Dave Sharpe letters Irene Lee production Kirk & Guru cover
Nathan Cosby assistant editor Mark Paniccia editor Joe Quesada editor in chief Dan Buckley publisher

I can't tell why they're here, unless merely to scare people to death!
They're emitting other frequencies as they talk, like insects.
Bruce, my helmet will break this down so you can translate with the Quinjet's computer.
Roger that, Ant-Man.
Sorry, visitors, but I'm breaking up this fun "Earthling Tag" game you're playing. Now stand still.

The enormous lady said stay still!
Hey!
Enormous, yet ***perfectly proportioned for her scaled-up size*** lady, I mean.

Ant-Man! We've got a rough translation of what they've been saying, I'll play it through the ship's speakers.
Stop running! We have something important to ask you! Stop!
So they weren't attacking. Glad I didn't stomp them.
I do not understand, you are all so simple! How could you have stopped it?
Simple?
Their females can grow to gargantuan size-- perhaps that is how they did it!
Agh! That one is emitting a sticky waste product upon us! We are trapped in its filth!
You know, I'm not feeling particularly helpful to these guys.
Okay, I've made adjustments-- we should be able to communicate directly with the aliens.
Can't wait.

What is this threat you speak of? How can we help?
The savages can translate our language! Perhaps they are not completely useless!
Grrr
Don't take it personally, this translation is far from perfect.
We are from the more advanced and civilized planetoid, Baston-Kar.
Unlike your world, we live in perfect health and harmony.
Did you just travel the cosmos to tell us how lame we are?
Then the other day we were visited by the harbinger of destruction...
...the SILVER SURFER.
Make the most of your final days for my master is coming soon.
The Eater of Worlds...
GALACTUS.
We heard that the only planet Galactus has ever spared is yours! Some group convinced him to leave by presenting a rare weapon...
The Ultimate Nullifier--in the hands of a human!
That was the Fantastic Four!

Though it disgusts us to do so, we must ask your help. Can you bring this weapon to our world to repel the destroyer?
I'm afraid we can't--if I may project my understanding of that day through your holographer. Unless I heard wrong...
...the Fantastic Four gave it to Galactus.
Here ya go, G. Now go on, git!
Okay, I don't know exactly what was said. But he took it in agreement to never eat our planet.
Then there is no hope.
At least we shall die without the indignity of having been helped by Earthmen.
Let us return--perhaps we can evacuate some of the population in time.
Yeah, good luck with that. Later.
Wait. These people came a long way to ask for our help--more or less--and they deserve it!
Ooh! Cap's going to make a speech!
Finally! He hasn't made a speech the whole time I've been a member!

Earth ingenuity and know-how saved our world from Galactus.
Actually I think the Watcher lent that Nullifier...
Yet should we not try to save another planet from the same threat?
Sure the Baston-Karians are rude jerks, but that doesn't mean they don't have the right to exist, just as we do. I know I won't be able to sleep knowing I didn't do my best to keep their world from being converted to caloric energy for an ancient being.
So I say let's go get the deep-space Quinjet and give it our best shot!
YEEEAAAAHHHH!!!
That really wasn't one of his better ones.
Yeah but still.

Within the hour:
Wow! This wormhole the aliens created has us halfway across the galaxy already!
I was actually hoping we'd take a longer way to give us more time to brainstorm.
Positive thoughts, team. We always come through somehow.

That sun no doubt possesses nutrients, master.
You need not point out every celestial body we pass, my herald.
You know nothing restores my vast life-forces like the life-forces of countless others.
Must you ever try to distract me from my prime imperative of consuming worlds?
It was but a suggestion, mighty Galactus.
You know I prefer non-obliteration alternatives.
Still. I have found you a world with a ruling species of eight billion and much flora and fauna.
You warned them of my approach, did you not.
Yes. I believe they deserve time to prepare for their end, even this race.
They are the worst-regarded people in this arm of the galaxy. At least they will not be missed.

We are here to help you repel Galactus.
We are truly doomed!
So they're all like that.
Hey, they've got ants!
Bigger than ours, but very similar. Fascinating!
You might want to save a couple then. Just sayin'.
Okay, here's my plan. We try to quickly find the nicest representative of every species on this planet and sample their DNA.
Then after Galactus drinks the planet dry, we'll terraform--
We can't plan to lose, that's not how you go into battle!
YOU MUST PLAN TO LOSE.

FOR YOU ALREADY HAVE. THIS WORLD'S FINAL DAY HAS COME...
BY THE HAND OF GALACTUS, DEVOURER OF WORLDS.
Avengers--
--ASSEMBLE!!!

KRACCK
You know we have to resist you, Silver Surfer!
I believe this is called shooting the messenger.
My master has already begun the process, it cannot be stopped.
His elemental converter will be complete in minutes.
Perhaps we can channel another energy source to it...
My readings show a-- OW!
Sorry, Bruce, that's enough thinking. We need your party animal side now.
Why did you--
--shoot webs--
--in HULK'S EYE!
RRRAAARRRH!!!

Oh sorry, man. Galactus' machine made my aim go all bad!!!
Hulk crush stupid machine!!
Earthmen? You should know my machines will rebuild themselves within minutes. Stop delaying progress.
BABLAAMMM!
BLOOOOM!
Then we'll keep hitting it, won't we, Hulk?
You never learn. Once again, I must unleash--
--The Punisher!
I thought it was going to be a guy in a skull shirt.
Hey shorty!
Eat some Whea--
--aw, he's already shredded through! And this is my special space-webbing!

Robot stop dancing! Hulk hate stupid arm dance.
KAWOOOM
Good work, Hulk!
Galactus will be displeased!
Even more so...
...by this!
WHHHHOOMMM
AH!!! I--hit by the Power Cosmic?!
Unthinkable!

It is always Earth people.
No one else ever gives me this much trouble. So be it.
I shall expend the energy to stop you.
RRRGHH!!
This is it-- I can do nothing to this cocoon!
He overlooked me, gang! Which kinda hurts my self-esteem, but don't worry. I'll go try to stop him with the Quinjet!
Forget that, Spider-Man. There's only one thing that will stop him, and I have it.
Because Galactus is so confident of his reputation, his ship is completely unguarded against small insignificant threats like me and these ants. That's how I was able to find...
The ULTIMATE NULLIFIER!
Ooh, FACE!

Check it out, G.
Now beat it and don't let the solar system hit you on the way out!
This gambit will not work again.
The Watcher guided your people to it out of desperation.
And I was surprised to see so powerful a device left to chance.
Even they knew it was too dangerous to remain in human hands. Activating it would end life as you understand it for light years around.
An alternative you cannot enact is no threat at all.
Now return the device that you dare not use.
CLICK

Why did you press that? You could have annihilated the universe!
I'm not sure he didn't.
Maybe if it were called the Ultimate Annihilator, but it's not. I think it's a Quantum Nullifier, and I've read a lot about how that would work in theory.
It would level the playing field by changing probability-- size and power wouldn't matter.
Everything would have equal likelihood of affecting anything else.
You are correct, though I scarcely believed your minds could conceive of such concepts.
Yet it is not my great power that makes me the universe's highest life-form. I shall meet any challenge you pose...and win.
Then let's test that.

I propose a game of strategy.
I accept.
Her always want to play that.
Aw man. I know where this is going.
LATER...
Knight Ant-Man, move to King's Bishop 4.
I *knew* we were going to be used as pieces.
I'm a queen.
LATER STILL...
It appears we are in "stalemate."
I could have won if Hulk hadn't gone too far earlier.
Hulk thought Rook always move whole length of board!
Shall we begin again?
I can think of a challenge that's fair *and* engaging.
No! Less boring!
Batter up!

Okay, team, I think we got them. They only have two guys, and we have Giant-Girl in the outfield.
I'm shortstop.
Nnnh!
CRACK
Wow!
PAP!
Up and down. Next!
Whew. He's even intimidating on a ball field.
He's pointing to Arcturus, Janet! Go way back!

Throw him some junk, A!
Think, think!
Okay!
Hank, what kind of pitch was that?
I call it Zeno's Paradoxer.
Space and Time are infinitely divisible, so the ball has to cross the halfway point to get there. But first the halfway point of that distance, and the half mark of that one...
Okay, Hank ruined that game. Any other scenarios?
I know one.

The game is Texas Hold 'em. I'll be the dealer.
Man, the Surfer has a serious poker face.
Hit me.
Why is it all Texas Hold 'em these days? What about five card stud?
Move! Shiny man want to be hit!
He means he wants another card!
Storm will win. She have all the pretty cards with people.
HULK! Arghh!
I move we take a break to recoup and come up with a better, more intuitive scenario that won't fall apart so easily.
I'm hungry.
Don't bring up--

...hunger. Now what?
Duh. Obviously we're in an infinite-star restaurant.
I'm afraid you've given them the perfect opportunity.
Oh no, you're right!
Good evening.
Our specials tonight are: Grilled Omicron Ceti-3, Smoked Lavaworld of the Myrrax Quadrant, Baston-Kar, ionized and magma-stewed, Orion Prime, nova-broiled with a side of moon.
Hmm... Baston-Kar sounds appetizing...
My friend who eats here all the time says the Lavaworld is the *best.*
Really? But it looks so... unpopulated.
I'll try it, but I'm hungry enough to eat *two* entrees.
Pretty sneaky, Surfer.
But we'll come up with another reality to thwart this.
I would not, Spider-Man.

Shiny Man threaten friend!
No, giant. I am saying to let this eventuality play out.
I think you may have given us the solution to our dilemma.
It sounds like you may sympathize with us.
That I do. I became Galactus' herald in trade to save my own world. I have tried to spare inhabited planets and convince him to gather energy from others, to no avail.
My hope now is that in a different context...
Waiter. Waiter!
I request the recipe for this from the chef. Are there more planetoids this delicious?
There are many more! I will gladly bring you to them.
It worked!
My energy levels are restored!
How about that? He was just so set in his ways that it was hard for him to change.
Well he is the oldest man in the universe.
Now that doomsday is averted...

...we can get back to our good ol' unchanging universe.
CLICK
It is just as before. Good work.
You feel pretty comfortable with that machine, huh?
It only has two buttons, what else could it do?
Here come the happy citizens.
World's all saved!
Why did it take you so long?
What was that strange effect that interrupted broad-casting? That was very inconvenient!
Why are you still here? You are finished saving our world, are you not?
So It's going to take us a little longer to get home since the aliens wouldn't open a wormhole for us to leave.
Maybe we should have let Galactus have one last lunch on his old diet...
THE END

#27

WEATHER GODDESS. PINT-SIZED SCIENTIST. SPIDER-POWERED WEB-SLINGER. SUPER-STRONG ALTER EGO OF SCIENTIST BRUCE BANNER GIANT-SIZED CRIMEFIGHTER. TOGETHER THEY ARE THE WORLD'S MIGHTIEST HEROES, BATTLING THE FOES THAT NO SINGLE SUPER HERO COULD WITHSTAND!
THE AVENGERS
AVENGERS ASSEMBLE--
SOOOO-WHEEEEE!!!
Ingredients: Jeff Parker-bacon, Ig Guara-ham, Sandro Ribeiro-ribs Guillem Mari-pork chop, Dave Sharpe-chitlins, Kirk & Guru-pig feet, Paul Acerios-went to market, Nathan Cosby-stayed home, Mark Paniccia-had roast beef, Joe Quesada-had none, Dan Buckley-went "Wee! Wee! Wee!"
100% SALTED PORK
STORM
ANT-MAN
SPIDER-MAN
HULK
GIANT-GIRL
Columbus, Mississippi.
$1
Now, why are we judges at a county fair again?
Hulk see all your movies!
?
Captain America thought it would build trust and goodwill with rural America.
You'll notice he isn't here today.
This pie is clearly the blue ribbon. Or maybe that blackberry one...

See, it takes the corn mashin's, and makes it inta gas for yer truck!
I don't think this is exactly a new invention, Farmer Dan...
But I'll investigate your "computerized burner" to see if it qualifies for the science contest.
Dark down here, gotta remember to bring a flashlight with me when I shrink. Hmm...
DROOP
Hey, these are just alarm clock parts stuck on with tar! Well this thing certainly isn't going to win...
BLOOP
Eh?
ZZZZZTT
FSSSHH

Come on back here, Eustace!
Argh! If I'd been inside, I'd be Giant-Girl-sized right now. Sorry everyone, I'll get it back to normal, hold on.
Were we expecting rain?
WWEEGGH!
WWEEGGH!
That sticky junk has clogged the matrix... come on...
Why Hulk in dark?
Oh shoot, that wasn't supposed to do that.
This sounds precarious, perhaps we should go outside.
Have the fireworks started already? Those look pretty!
Not in the daytime--would they?
--eyes aren't adjusted...
Yeah, everything looks funny... kind of...

...BIG.
Um...okay. Let me just get this cleaned out and try it again. Don't go anywhere or I'll lose you.
Ha! Ant-Man made self big by accident. Stupid Ant-Man!
No, Hulk, it's *us* who got small!
Eustace!
Interesting to see how Ant-Man views the world.
Interesting to see a wad of chewing gum that big.
Eustace, stop, dang it!
Look out!
Piggy in the middle!
Yay! Hulk's friend want hug!

That not hug.
Piggie?
TROMP
Who step on Hulk?!
I don't see him...
Eeyah!
There he is!
Hulk! Put that man down!

Aha, got it back to normal.
Just a sec, team, now I'll be able to--
WHEEEG WHEEEG
Hey! Come back with that equipment!
WHEEEG
WHEEEG
WHEEEG
Storm! We've got to get my helmet back from that pig!
Spider-Man! The rest of you retrieve the helmet--and quick--
--what dissolves cotton candy?
Spit!
Come on, Hulk! We have to catch the pig!
Pig owe Hulk a hug!
Uh, yeah!

WHEEEG!
WHEEEG!
WHEEEG!
He's up there by those cloggers!
Boy, that pig can move, huh?
NO! It's always been my darkest fear that I'd meet death by line-dancing!
Watch out!
They're dosey-doing!
Oof!
There, behind that stand! We'll get him now!
Let's take the high road and come down in front of him!
Ha! Catch little piggie now!

OW!
PING
PING
Stop! I'm not a sweet little duck!
And why are you shooting at sweet little ducks, anyway?
PING
BANG
BANG
This thing is rigged! You'll never win that cabbage patch doll!
What luck! He's running into that petting zoo!
Now we've got him!
I can't see, everyone's in my way! You two cover the ground.
The heck with this.
I'll cover more ground this way.
That look like fun! Hulk want turn!
BA-GOCK!

SNORT
Hey donkey! Give Hulk ride like chicken!
TUG
TUG
TUG
YEEHAW!
WHOCK
Ow...
Sorry, Hulk.
Hulk see pig! Pig at other gate!
Thanks big guy! Little big guy.
Okay! I can corral him into this pen if you can close the door!
I completely forgot that I can still grow, duh.
I'll lock up that swine!
Huh, not as big as I hoped. Nnngh...
Every little bit helps, Knee-High Girl.
THWIP
THWIP

WHEEG!
Glad to have that off, huh? My pleasure.
Now we need to let Ant-Man know where we are somehow.
Hulk, jump up and yell for Ant--
--hey kid, let go!
Look mama, a dolly!
Step right up! Let's see who the strongest man in Lowndes County is!
Hulk strongest there is! Give Hulk that!
Uh...do what?
WHAM
HA!
RINGGGGGGGGGGGG
What....
I think they're over there.

Whew, it's in one piece.
Every-one get under it and I'll Pym-particle you back to normal.
THWIP
Wait--while I'm at this size and can do some finesse work...
Later...
Ah.
Boy, Hank, I don't know how you can stand being that little so often.
I like it. I get uncomfortable with people staring at me in costume.
Like anyone's paying attention to us--
--it's all about that pig.
THIS PIG IS REALL HARD TO CATCH
Why does everyone think the pig is so great instead of the spider who wrote the message?
You want a ribbon for writing now?
Some End!

Meanwhile, in N.Y.C...
At last my journey is ended!
This planet is suitable to be enslaved by
KRAGE
the Conqueror!

From my spaceship my robo-minions will march!
From these streets my army will flow outward like a crashing wave!

Arise! Awaken! Step forth my robot army!
Krage the Conqueror commands you!

And when Krage commands, it is for all others to...
...eh?

And Some OTHER Small Problems
PAUL TOBIN WRITER JACOPO CAMAGNI PENCILER
TROY HUBBS AND NORMAN LEE INKERS
ULISES ARREOLA COLORIST
DAVE SHARPE LETTERER
PAUL ACERIOS PRODUCTION
NATHAN COSBY ASSISTANT EDITOR
MARK PANICCIA EDITOR
JOE QUESADA EDITOR IN CHIEF
DAN BUCKLEY PUBLISHER
CAPTAIN AMERICA.
Oh. You Earthlings looked a lot smaller on the viewer.
IRON MAN.
Put him in a box or something, will you, Cap? I've got to check in with the others.

Wolverine? You there?
Yeah... it's me.
Good. Iron Man, here. Everything okay on your end?

Just the usual state fair joy. Hulk caught a pig.
I'll assume you're joking.
How's practice going? Have they spotted you yet?

Give me some credit. I'm a world-class sneaky ninja type.
The ultimate master of disguise.
I'M WOLVERINE KICK ME!
Eustace?
Well, have fun spying on your friends.
It's not spying. It's practice.
Yeah. Spy practice. Okay... I should go.
Any problems?
Nope. Everything's all boxed up. How are the rest of the Avengers doing?
Hulk apparently found a pig. That's about it.

Shouldn't we be giving the alien over to a special agency?
Not necessary. New York cops can handle it. They've seen everything.
Thanks.
NYPD

There's my phone again. Probably Wolverine letting me know the Hulk won a pie-eating contest.
Can't be. After last year, they banned the Hulk from entering any of the--

ARE YOU BALD?!! LADIES DON'T LIKE THE CHROME-DOMES! HIT REPLY TO GET GO-GROW HAIR PRODUCT!
That's... loud.
ARE YOU BALD?!! LADIES DON'T LIKE THE--

What was that?
Spam call. Getting them a lot lately.
Oh, those. I get them too. Dating chat lines. Teeth whitening. And... other stuff.
CLICK

They're very irritating. Somebody should do something about them.
First e-mails, now cell phones. What next? It has to end.

I'm not going to worry about it *today*. I'm too happy to have a day off.
Would be kind of fun to watch Hulk chase a pig, though.
Not if you happen to be a *pig*.

Still, if you want to head out to the fair, we could.
Not a chance. I'd rather shoot some hoops. Get a *workout* in.
GANDER'S GYM
Ganders Gym — members only
GYM

Soon...
Two points!
Good shot! Now we're tied up.

Only because you spotted me *twenty points.*
True. But I made you take your *armor* off.

After I win, you want to get a burger somewhere?
Sure. I know a nice place that--

I AM HEIR TO THE GOODNABE OIL FORTUNE! I CALL BECAUSE I TRUST YOU! MONEY OPPORTUNITY!
I MUST WIRE TWENTY MILLION DOLLARS TO AMERICA AND YOU CAN HELP BY SUPPLYING YOUR BANK ACCOUNT NUMBER AND--
ZOOP
Sorry. I didn't think I left that on.
Nothing like a little fee-fraud scheme to interrupt a game.

Now, where were we? I was up by three, right?
Tied. And I had the ball. Who's scheming now?
Hey, I need all the edge I can get. Can I put on just a few pieces of my armor?
The jet boots maybe?
Finish this game and we can--
WEIGHT AWAY! BUY WEIGHT AWAY! HAVING TROUBLE ON STAIRS? TOO BUSY FOR EXERCISE? AMAZING NEW PILL!
WEIGHT AWAY! WEIGHT AWAY! DIAL REPLY AND YOU WILL--

That's it! My phone was off!
Can you trace the calls?
Easily. Just let me jack my phone card into my armor.
And then we can run these spammers into the ground. I should've done this long ago.
Soon. Sixty-five blocks away...
The calls are coming from here? I figured we'd have to go to Russia. The Ukraine. The Skrull Homeworld.
Nope. Here. I'm sure of it.

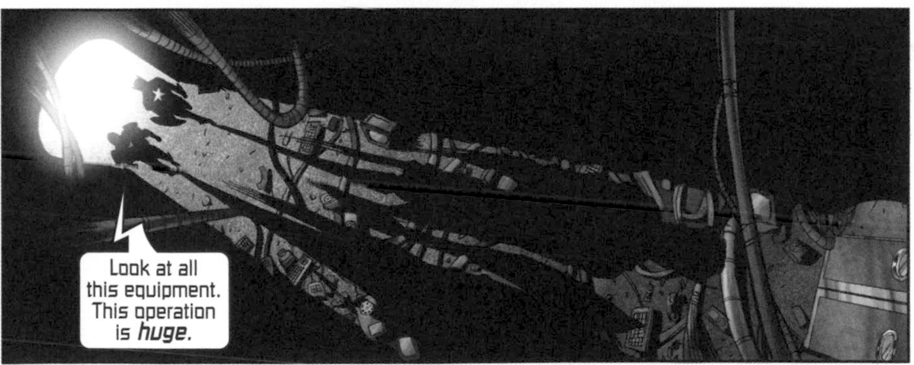
Look at all this equipment. This operation is huge.

Here we are. The telephone throne room.
Who are those guys?

Excuse me.
Busy makin' money. Put the coffee on the table, the pizza on my lap, and the bill on my tab.
No, we're here to make a complaint.
Eee-yeeps! Guys! It's the Iron Man!!
An' he gots Captain America with him!
Well, those two owlhoots is about to get learned a lesson!
That's right! Compliments of...
THE ENFORCERS!

Fancy Dan! Judo expert!
Watch my footwork! If you can!
I'm Montana. Expert with a lasso!
Ain't nothing what can escape my lariat.
I'm Ox. Strong. Care to meet some real muscle, Iron Man?

So the Hulk gets a pig, and we get these guys. Who wins?
That would be a toss-up.

Fancy Dan strikes!
Is Fancy Dan kidding?

KRRTHUDD
Oh cripes!

Ox!
On my way!!
Cap, this one's *mine.* I need to feel better after the *basketball debacle.*

THUDDNIKK
Owwww! Dang! What're you *made* of?
Honestly, I think *my name* gives it away.

Gufff!!

Yee-haw! Ol' Montana done caught himself an *Iron Man!*

So what? Cap...hit him.
Can do.
Awww. Shoot fire.

Twenty Minutes Later...
That's, lessee, 12,645,243 counts of fraud.
Add that to your wholesale breaking of the no-call lists and the phone-tapping charges, and you boys are looking at one lengthy jail term.

Our job here is done. Let's get that burger.
I don't think I've ever felt more heroic.

Hope the accommodations are fancy enough for ya, Fancy Dan.
Take it easy! And don't I get a phone call?
Haw! Ain't you made enough phone calls?

Sigh

So...my name's Krage.
What'd they get you for?
POLICE